KIDS' SPORT STORIES

KEEP DANCING

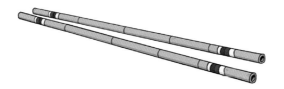

by Cristina Oxtra

illustrated by Seb Burnett

raintree

Raintree is an imprint of Capstone Global Library Limited, a company incorporated in England and Wales having its registered office at 264 Banbury Road, Oxford, OX2 7DY – Registered company number: 6695582

www.raintree.co.uk
myorders@raintree.co.uk

ISBN 978 1 3982 1494 1

Designed by Kyle Grenz
Originated by Capstone Global Library Ltd
Printed and bound in India

British Library Cataloguing in Publication Data
A full catalogue record for this book is available from the British Library.

CONTENTS

Glossary

 **athlete** someone who is well-trained in a sport

 **bamboo** a hot-weather grass with a hard, hollow stem

 **Philippines** a country in South-east Asia; people from there are called Filipinos

 **tinikling** a dance from the Philippines that features bamboo poles

Chapter 1
DO YOU DANCE?

Lito and his twin sister, Nenita, were waiting for their dad to pick them up from school. When the car came, Nenita ran towards it.

"Hurry, Lito!" she shouted. "We'll be late for our dance class!"

A group of boys heard Nenita.

"Do you dance?" one of them asked Lito, laughing.

The other boys started laughing too.

"My sister dances," Lito said. "I have to go and watch."

Lito hurried to the car. He got in the back seat with his sister and pulled the door shut.

"I heard what you said to those boys. You lied, Lito," Nenita said, frowning at him. "You dance as well."

Lito didn't say anything.

"Why did you lie about dancing?"
Nenita asked. "It's fun, and you're really
good at it."

"I don't want to talk about it," he said.
"You wouldn't understand anyway."

"What's going on back there?" Dad asked.

Before Nenita could answer, Lito said, "Nothing."

He and his sister travelled to dance class without another word.

Chapter 2
FALLING DOWN

At their lesson, Lito and Nenita took off their shoes and socks and changed their clothes. They walked onto the dance floor. Two other kids were sitting on the floor, facing each other. Each one held the ends of two long bamboo poles.

Lito and Nenita's dance group did dances from the Philippines. Lito and Nenita had been practising the tinikling. Soon they were going to perform this special dance at their school's spring festival.

"Ready to dance?" the teacher asked.

"Yes!" the kids yelled – except Lito.

The music started. The two kids with the poles tapped them on the floor twice. Then they clapped the poles together. They did this again and again.

Tap, tap, clap! Tap, tap, clap!

Lito and Nenita hopped between the moving poles. Tinikling dancers copy the way a tikling bird hops through the grass. As the music speeds up, so do the poles.

Tap, tap, clap! Tap, tap, clap!

Lito was usually quick on his feet. But not today. He tripped and fell to the floor.

"Are you OK, Lito?" the teacher asked.

"I'm fine," Lito said, rubbing his foot.

"I just need to sit down for a minute."

Lito sat down on a bench next to his dad.

"What's wrong, Lito?" Dad asked.

"You're not yourself today."

"I can't dance at the festival, Dad," Lito said. "The boys at school will make fun of me. They play sports. They're athletes. I should be an athlete, not a dancer."

"Lito, you work hard on your dancing skills. You are strong and quick," Dad said. "You already *are* an athlete!"

"Am I?" said Lito.

"How do you feel when you dance?"
Dad asked.

Lito thought for a moment. "Happy,"
he said. "I'm Filipino, and I dance. I'm
showing people who I am and how great
Filipino dances are."

"And that's all that matters," his dad said. "Keep dancing, Lito. I'm proud of you."

Chapter 3
FESTIVAL TIME

It was the day of the school festival. The show was about to start. Lito peeked out from backstage.

"Those boys are here," he told Nenita.

"Don't be scared, Lito," Nenita said. "Show them who you are!"

The boys laughed as Lito stepped onstage with Nenita.

The music started. The two kids with the poles tapped them on the floor twice. Then they clapped the poles together.

Tap, tap, clap! Tap, tap, clap!

Lito and Nenita began hopping between the moving poles. Lito tucked his arms behind him. Nenita held the sides of her skirt. The pair turned to the right and to the left. They spun round and round. They didn't miss a step.

Next, Lito took his sister's hand. Together, they skipped and twirled between the poles.

Nenita then stepped aside and left Lito on his own. The music played a little faster, and the poles moved faster too.

Tap, tap, clap! Tap, tap, clap!

Lito's knees pumped up and down. He was dancing well. When the music sped up again, the poles really tapped and clapped!

Tap, tap, clap! Tap, tap, clap!

Lito's toes brushed up against a pole.

He wobbled, but he didn't fall.

"Go, Lito!" Nenita shouted.

Lito breathed hard. His legs hurt. But he kept dancing. It looked like his feet weren't even touching the floor.

The boys in the front row stared, their mouths open. They were not laughing anymore. They were amazed!

Lito took Nenita's hand. They jumped and twirled between the bamboo poles again.

When the music stopped, Lito and Nenita stopped. They raised their arms high into the air.

The crowd cheered. Lito and Nenita's parents stood up and yelled. The boys at the front clapped. One even gave a thumbs-up. Lito and Nenita bowed.

"Now, aren't you glad you kept dancing?" Nenita asked.

"I certainly am!" Lito said with a big smile.

JUMPING OVER THORNS

This is a Filipino game called Luksong Tinik, or Jumping Over Thorns. Tinikling dancers must be quick and light on their feet. Practise your jumping skills with this fun game. The goal is to jump over the other team's feet and hands (the "thorns") without touching them.

What you need:
- at least three friends
- space to run and jump

What you do:
1. Split into two teams, Team A and Team B.
2. Two players from Team A are the base. They sit on the ground with the bottoms of their feet touching.
3. Players on Team B take turns jumping over the feet.
4. Once everyone on Team B has jumped, the base players add more "thorns". One base puts a right hand on top of their feet (palm out with the little finger touching a foot). The other base stacks his/her right hand on top of the first hand. Palms should face out and the hands should be stacked little finger to thumb.
5. Team B takes turns jumping again. If everyone on Team B clears the thorns, the base players add another hand on top of the first one.
6. Repeat steps 4 and 5 until someone on Team B touches the thorns. Then the teams swap places and start again.

REPLAY IT

Have another look at this picture. How do you think Lito felt as he walked onto the stage? How would you feel if you were in that same position?

Now pretend you are Lito. Write a letter to your grandparents telling them all about your dance at the festival.

ABOUT THE AUTHOR

Cristina Oxtra is a Filipino American author. She earned an MFA in creative writing for children and young adults at Hamline University in the US. She is a recipient of the Loft Literary Center's 2019-2020 Mirrors & Windows Fellowship for indigenous writers and writers of colour.

ABOUT
THE ILLUSTRATOR

Seb Burnett is an illustrator and game developer living in Bristol. When not drawing he loves going for long walks through the woods and hunting for monsters. He hasn't found any yet.